4APurpose Enterprises

presents

A Forgiver's Consequences

By

Edwin De Leon

This is a work of fiction. The author has invented the characters. Any resemblance to actual persons, living or dead, is purely coincidental.

Order this book online at www.trafford.com/07-1203
or email orders@trafford.com

Most Trafford titles are also available at major online book retailers.

Note for Librarians: A cataloguing record for this book is available from Library and Archives Canada at www.collectionscanada.ca/amicus/index-e.html

ISBN: 978-1-4251-3231-6

Illustrated by Jose Pagan
Cover Design/Artwork by Jose Pagan
Photography by Sonya Arletta Finley www.sa-creatives.com

We at Trafford believe that it is the responsibility of us all, as both individuals and corporations, to make choices that are environmentally and socially sound. You, in turn, are supporting this responsible conduct each time you purchase a Trafford book, or make use of our publishing services. To find out how you are helping, please visit www.trafford.com/responsiblepublishing.html

Our mission is to efficiently provide the world's finest, most comprehensive book publishing service, enabling every author to experience success. To find out how to publish your book, your way, and have it available worldwide, visit us online at www.trafford.com/10510

www.trafford.com

North America & international
toll-free: 1 888 232 4444 (USA & Canada)
phone: 250 383 6864 • fax: 250 383 6804
email: info@trafford.com

The United Kingdom & Europe
phone: +44 (0)1865 722 113 • local rate: 0845 230 9601
facsimile: +44 (0)1865 722 868 • email: info.uk@trafford.com

10 9 8 7 6 5 4 3 2 1

Dedications

First, this book is dedicated to God, to whom I give all the praise and glory!

Thank you for being my all, my Alpha and Omega!

To my mother, Maria Esther Castro, my father Eulalio De Leon Sr., and my sister Hilda. I miss you all so very much. I weep in your absence, but I find solace in knowing that you are all in a better place.

To my son; it is my responsibility to leave you with a legacy and inheritance that you can be proud of, that you can benefit from and pass on to your children. Therefore, I am trying to do all I can to meet that obligation. I love you.

Acknowledgements

To my other siblings: I love you all. Thank you for your support and prayers. To my nieces and nephews: grab the baton and take it to the next level.

To my extended *Familia* in my patriarch land of *El Boriquen*, que Dios me los bendiga! To my city of birth, New York, I assure you that I have not forgotten where I'm from. To my wonderful family in Chicago and elsewhere throughout the country, I hope to see you soon! To my friends, associates, and all of those I meet along the way: thank you for the relationships we forge and the experiences we share. Lastly, but definitely not least, to all my readers and supporters – thank you, and may God bless you!.

To my future, I look forward to experiencing you, in God's will.

To all

My accomplishments are not there to impress you, no more then my failures are there to discourage you, but instead to inspire you. For I was born with many natural odds against me, but all supernatural odds for me. And the purpose of my existence is not to impress, but to impress upon you, that with God all things are possible.

Edwin

I knew you, and before you were born I consecrated you; I have appointed you a prophet to the nations (Jeremiah 1:5 NASB)

A Prophet Once Said to Me

Entregate a él Senor y ve adelante mi hijo, y tu verás que él hará contingo grandes cosas. Y él te tomará lugares que tu nunca te imaginado."

Translation: "Go forth and surrender to God my son, and you will see that he will do with you great things. And he will take you places you never imagined."

Maria Esther De Leon Castro-My Mother

Exert from my last conversation with my mother, hours before she went with the Lord.

It was 9:15 am on Monday, when Joyce looked towards Lisa Fontaine's desk and noticed that she had not arrived. Lisa was known for her punctuality and professionalism and her recent tardiness had Joyce very concerned. Not to mention, there would be her supervisor's disapproval to face. Joyce was Lisa's coworker and a friend of Joyce's as well. Lisa was a beautiful young woman. Though she was petite in stature, her features were striking; she wore her hair long so that it framed her eyes, which were like chestnut-painted windows. Her skin, youthful and flawless, blazed with a beautiful bronze tone.

Lisa obviously did not have a problem attracting men and they always seemed to possess similar traits and characteristics. They tended to be handsome, financially secure, and, unfortunately, extremely controlling and jealous. Lisa's husband, David, was no exception.

David Fontaine was not only controlling and jealous, but was prone to violence as well. He had struck Lisa several times, but she continued to forgive him and refused to leave. Though his reputation for violence preceded him, Lisa completely ignored it, believing that he could change and that things would be different between them.

With growing concern, Joyce decided to call Lisa. Therefore, she rose from her chair and found a secluded area where she could have some privacy. She pressed one on her cell phone, and the phone began to ring. On the other end, a female with a groggy voice answered the phone.

"Hello..." the groggy voice said.

"Lisa... Lisa, is this you?!" Joyce asked, whispering.

"Yes... Joyce?" Lisa asked.

"Yes, girl, where are you?!" Joyce asked desperately.

"I'm home… uh… why? Wait…what time is it?" Lisa asked, confused.

"Girl, it's almost 9:30 and you're late again!" Joyce exclaimed.

"Oh my God, you're kidding, right?!" Lisa asked with concern.

"No I'm not!" Joyce responded sharply. "Lisa, what is going on? This is becoming a pattern for you, and it's not like you!" Joyce said with a raised tone.

"Okay… Okay… don't shout; I have a severe headache. Plus, I get enough of that at home!" Lisa responded sharply.

"I bet you do," Joyce said, in a low, sarcastic tone.

"Excuse me, what did you say?!" Lisa asked in a defensive tone. That was rare for Lisa, but she had been very edgy lately, and her tolerance level was extremely low. Especially when anyone started talking about her husband.

David was a very successful lawyer whom Lisa had met while working as a legal aide at the same law firm where he worked. Moreover, the minute she laid her eyes on him, she was enticed, everything she always wanted: intelligent, successful, and extremely handsome. His success became such that he was able to open his own practice, and his notoriety had garnered him great respect in the community. However, some argued that this respect was really more fear than anything else – his success had garnered him not only wealth, but power as well. Unfortunately, the fairly tale marriage that Lisa envisioned had evolved into a nightmare. However, Lisa continued to make excuses for his behavior. In addition, she defended him against all critics, including her friends and family.

"I knew it, Lisa – its David again, isn't it?" Joyce asked boldly.

This question did not sit well with Lisa, and it received a swift and admonishing response. "I've told you before, and I'm going to say it one last time, keep David's name out of your mouth! You are a friend and I love you, but I will not allow you to talk badly about my husband! If it's not you, it's Javier, or my family – DAMN! I'm sick and tired of everyone being in my business! He is a good man; he's just under a lot of pressure!" Lisa cried, in an angry, escalating tone. Joyce, remembering she was at work and considering her friend's current emotional state, reluctantly remained silent. Then, after a brief respite, she responded.

"You know what… you're right… it's your life, and he's your husband. I'm sorry, Lisa. And I promise not to intervene again… I have to get back to work Lisa, but I will pray that…" Joyce said, and began to weep.

"Joyce... Joyce, listen, I'm sorry... I'm really sorry. Please don't be upset. I just had a horrible weekend and I... I don't know what to do. My life is a mess, and I don't know what to do," Lisa said, beginning to weep profusely.

Joyce, quickly began to console and reassures her friend. "You don't deserve this, Lisa, and you don't have to put up with it. And if you don't want your friends and family in your business, there are other options," Joyce said.

"I know," Lisa responded softly.

"Look...I know you love him, but David has issues you can't help him with. You cannot do God's work. And he keeps telling you he's going to seek help, but he never does!" Joyce said, with escalating emotion. But there was only silence in response. "Lisa...did he hit you again?" Joyce asked hesitantly. Again, there was no response. "You know, my friend still works for the Battered Women Shelter, and she can help you!." Joyce said pleadingly.

Again, there was no response, and the silence was so deafening you could hear a pin drop. "Lisa!?...Lisa!?" Joyce exclaimed. However, Lisa was obviously entrenched in the moment and in deep thought. And just when Joyce was about to call her again, Lisa responded. "I have to go Joyce... sorry... I love him, you don't understand... bye." Lisa said, before abruptly hanging up.

Joyce looked at her phone, and considered calling Lisa back, but she quickly realized that she had better get back to work. As she passed by Lisa's desk on the way back to her own, she heard the phone ringing. She stopped short and stared towards Lisa's desk reflectively. However, she quickly broke her stare, shook her head in concern, and continued towards her desk.

The phone stopped ringing and Lisa's answering machine came on. "Hi, you've reached the desk of Lisa Fontaine, please leave your name and number and I will gladly return your call". After a beep, a male voice came over the line. "Lisa, *hola muchacha!* you know who this is, haven't heard from you in a while, give your boy a call!" the voice said humorously, and hung up. It was Javier, Lisa's best friend and confidant from childhood.

Several hours later, Joyce arrived back to work from lunch. As she passed by Lisa's desk again, her eyes canvassed the area, hoping to find evidence of her arrival. Unfortunately, however, there was none. As Joyce slumped onto her chair in disappointment, she heard Lisa's phone ring again. Lisa's voicemail answered again, but this time, the caller did not leave a message.

Back at the Fontaines' home, Lisa, feeling disillusioned and extremely fatigued, lay down to take a nap. However, her nap was interrupted by the sound of her cell phone. She heard it ringing, but it was not within her reach. Still a bit incoherent from her nap and not really in the mood to speak to anyone, she ignored the call. However, she decided to get up and freshen up. She enters the bathroom in her master bedroom and reached for the toothbrush. She poured the toothpaste on her toothbrush and begins to brush her teeth. As she brushed her teeth, she looked in the mirror. She stared at herself and began to reflect on her life and her relationship with David. This reflection led to a profound and extensive discussion with herself.

Later Monday evening, the sunset was peeking through the windows of the Fontaine's home. And as Joyce suspected earlier, Lisa and David did have an altercation this weekend. Though it was not physical, it was volatile and verbally abusive. Lisa, in an effort to put the events of this weekend behind them, was preparing a delightful and romantic dinner. She had showered and dressed in a very sexy short black dress, with spaghetti straps. The length of it, or lack thereof, accentuated her beautiful toned legs. It was one of

David's favorites. In addition, she'd misted her smooth skin with some Burberry London perfume. Consequently, the aroma occupied every space she passed through, but in a very subtle manner.

David was a fitness fanatic, and consequently he was very particularly about his diet. So, always considerate of her husband's diet, Lisa was preparing a high-protein, low-fat, and low-carbohydrate meal – baked tarragon chicken, with Italian herbs and vegetables. The dining table was set and adorned with two beautiful white candles. In addition, to wet the palate, a nicely aged red wine was chilling on the table. In the backdrop, you could hear the smooth jazz sounds of acclaimed saxophonist Grover Washington Jr.

Lisa looked at the clock on the wall, and realized that it was almost time for David to arrive. Therefore, she quickly opened the oven to check if the chicken was ready. However, as she reached to grab the fork to turn the chicken over, she heard David's keys jiggling in the lock. Concerned about her lack of preparedness, she put the fork down and frantically adjusted her attire. David continued to struggle with the door's lock, which they had been having problems with lately. He had told Lisa to get it fixed, but she hadn't yet gotten around to it.

Always lacking in patience, David began to get irritated. "Lisa, open this damn door!" he demanded loudly. "I thought I told you to get this damn thing fixed," he said, banging on the door. As Lisa approached the door nervously, she looked up to the skies and whispered "Please, God, not again."

"Lisa!" he shouts again.

"Wait… I mean… I'm here, baby" she said carefully. When Lisa finally opened the door, she quickly noticed David's bellicose demeanor. Always the pacifist, she quickly approached him to greet him with a kiss. However, as her lips quickly approached his, he turned his face away. "Don't even think about it!" he said callously as he entered the house.

"Did I…did I not tell you to get this lock fixed?" he asked, trying to lower his tone.

"I'm sorry, baby, I just haven't had the chance to do it, but I promise… I will," she said, nervously apologetic.

"And I called you several times today, what you been doing?! You couldn't be that busy!" he said insinuatingly.

David would be infuriated if she told him that she failed to go to work again. She approached him again in another attempt to kiss and hug him. However, he nonchalantly turned and walked away. As he reached the stairs to go up to change, he looks towards her. "You know… I'm just sick of your promises, Lisa, can't you do anything right?!" he asked, shouting. "I'm going to shower and change – have my food ready by the time I come down. I hope you at least got that right!" he said threateningly as he walked swiftly up the stairs.

Extremely disappointed, Lisa quickly walked towards the kitchen, shaking visibly. "Hey!" David yelled. Lisa stopped in her tracks, but did not look back or respond. "Hey, I know you heard me!" he shouts. "Yes, David!" she said in a mocking tone, still not looking back.

"Excuse me?!" he asked in astonishment. He was obviously surprised with Lisa's tone – this was a tone seldom heard from her. "I advise you to watch your tone with me and look at me when I'm talking to you!" he said angrily, stepping towards her. Concerned about the repercussions, she quickly gave David her undivided attention. "Yes, David" she said in a low tone.

"You know what, just take that dress off and get rid of those candles, you have obviously ruined the evening – again!" he said angrily as he continued to walk upstairs. Just before he reached the top of the stairs, he shouted a parting shot: "And turn that damn music off!"

Lisa just stood there for a moment, absorbing the blow of his callousness and his harsh words. It was obvious that David was harboring some residual anger from this past weekend. Yet Lisa, exemplifying the ultimate patience, entered the kitchen to check on the food. However, when she opened the stove's door, she gasped in dismay. "Oh no!" she said, in astonished disappointment. The chicken had cooked too long and it had burned. At that moment, she threw her hands up and looked towards the heavens, shaking her head in despair. And, despite her best attempts to be strong, she began to weep. "What am I going to do – please help me, Lord," she whispered to the heavens, unable to stop sobbing uncontrollably.

She suddenly dropped to the floor and sits against the kitchen cabinets. Desperately trying to regain her composure and stop crying, she began to wipe her tears away frantically. With relentless determination, she sat there contemplating her options. She must immediately find something for David to eat, or else deal with his cantankerous attitude. Moreover, because of his *particular* diet, her options were not very vast. Suddenly, overwhelmed with emotions, she began to feel dizzy and nauseated. Unable to resist the compelling need to regurgitate, she stood over the sink and heaved. Feeling a bit relieved, yet exhausted, she slumped to the floor again.

Suddenly, she heard the shower turn off. Her stomach began to rattle with nerves as she glanced towards the stairs. "Think, Lisa, think!" she quickly shouted to herself. Suddenly, she remembered that David loved to patronize a particular Chinese restaurant near their home. So maybe, just maybe, she could convince him to go out for a nice romantic dinner and they could talk. At least it would be in a public place, and he would refrain from berating or striking her. Or, better yet, maybe she should order out. That would give her a chance to get some air, and maybe he would have calmed down by the time she got back. She quickly evaluated her options and decided on takeout. This expedient decision would surprise David; he had always accused her of being indecisive.

When she looked around for her cell phone, she quickly realized that it was upstairs in their bedroom. This placed her in a precarious situation, because she was hoping to place the order prior to engaging with him again. She looked at her house phone, but realized that the number was programmed on her cell phone. When she arrived at the steps, she paused, looking up the stairs. With extreme trepidation, she began to walk upstairs. With her eyes gazing at the steps, her body, weighted down with her somber mood, reached the top. And when she finally looks up, there, standing before her was David.

"Hey..." Lisa says, in a soft and submissive tone. She quickly looked at his eyes and posture, trying to evaluate his mood. To her surprise, his eyes seemed soft and inviting. In addition, his body seemed relaxed and passive. The only clothes he was wearing were some house pants and a tank top. "Hey... are we ready to eat?" he said cordially, rubbing his stomach. She hesitated to respond, hoping to capture this tranquil moment. At this very moment, she could see the man she had fallen so deeply in love with, from his flawless physical attributes to the calm demeanor he had exemplified when they were courting. Moreover, Lisa had truly believed at that time that whatever rumors existed about his nefarious behavior, they were grossly exaggerated.

"Lisa... hello... what are you staring at?" he asked, with a light chuckle. However, Lisa just put her head down in grave disappointment - she didn't want to have to inform him about dinner. David assumed that her silence was a direct result of the altercation they had just had. "Listen, about earlier, I'm... sorry, but you know I..."

She interrupted him quickly. "Baby... the food...I'm sorry... but the food... the chicken burned" she said quickly, slumping her head on his chest. "I had planned this whole elaborate and romantic dinner... for us, you know...so we can move on, baby... I'm tired of us fighting all the time," she said, as she began to weep on his chest.

David paused and stared at her with disbelief. He was willing to put the recent events behind them, but his patience was growing thin. David grabbed her by her arms and gently pushed her away from him. Her body tensed up as she looked at him with fear. It was a spontaneous reaction; she has felt the wrath of his hands and arms all too often. Just like that, David's demeanor changed drastically.

"You're kidding… right!?" he asked, while grinding his teeth and gripping her arms more tightly.

"But baby… listen… we can order some Chinese… and we can sit down… and eat and…" She tried to respond with a solution, but he interrupted her quickly. "You know what… I tried, Lisa… I've tried to be patient with you!" he yelled, raising his tone of voice. "What's going on?! Where's your head at?! Focus, woman! Damn!" he shouted, turning away and walking towards the bedroom. "David, please!" she said, pleading. However, David opened the closet and begins to pull some clothes out.

"Where are you going, baby?" she asked concerned.

"Look, don't baby me, and don't worry about it, okay?" he said sharply. As he began to put a pair of jeans on, Lisa made a failed attempt to approach him. However, he stopped her in her tracks. "I advise you not come any closer, and just leave me alone right now. I'm hungry, tired and pissed, so step off!" he said threateningly. Intimidated by his tone and by the conviction in his voice, Lisa quickly backed off. David finished dressing, grabbed his keys, and left, slamming the door behind him. Lisa was left standing there, totally mortified by what had just transpired. Her emotions were restrained until she heard his car speed off. Then the flow of tears from her eyes became uncontrollable.

David pulled into the parking lot of the Xing Ming Chinese restaurant – the exact restaurant where Lisa was intending to order the food. However, as he sits in his car, his hunger was suppressed by the anger boiling within him. He backed his car up, and sped off. As he sped down the street, his vindictive nature came to the fore; he began to contemplate ways to get back at Lisa. The Palace is a prestigious strip club, patronized by the elite clientele only. It was for members only, and the annual membership fees were in the thousands. It was a frequent outlet for David, especially when he and Lisa were at odds. As he entered the club, the two revealingly clad women who were staffing the door greeted him in unison. "Hello, Mr. Fontaine," they said, smiling.

"Hey!" David replied abruptly, walking by them.

"Hmmm, I wonder what's wrong with him?" one asked the other.

"Hey, you never know with him – he's been extremely moody lately," the other responded.

"I know, but girl, I don't care; he is so fine!" one said.

"I know, and he has money too!" the other replied with approval. They looked at each other and chuckled.

Meanwhile, Lisa was still distraught over what had just transpired. Therefore, in a feeble attempt to calm down, she undressed and got in the shower. This was a common practice of hers. She found to be very therapeutic, when she was stressed. Placing her head underneath the showerhead, she tilted her head back and allowed the cool water to flush her face and hair. At that moment, the water from the shower joined forces with the tears that continued to flow from her eyes. Consumed with emotions, she slumped to the base of the tub and sat there, crying uncontrollably.

David made his way to his usual table in an obscured corner of the club. As soon as he sat down, the waitress approached him. "Hey handsome, how are you tonight? The usual?" she asked.

"Look, you can save the pleasantries – and yes, bring me the usual" he said abrasively.

"What's wrong, baby? Having a bad day?" she said teasingly. However, David was in no mood to play. He stared her down with piercing eyes. Fully cognizant of whom she was dealing with, she quickly walked away.

Soon after the waitress walked away, David felt a pair of arms wrap around his shoulders. Edgy and irritated, he reacted reflexively and defensively. "What the…" he said.

"Hey baby, relax – it's just me, your, Diamond girl!" the woman said excitedly. David was one of her best-paying clients. She attempted to plant a kiss on lips, but he turned and gave her his cheek.

"Hey... what's up?" he replied somberly.

"Wow… that's all I get? What's wrong, baby?" she asked.

"You know what's wrong… same old stuff," he replied. Diamond was considered the premier dancer of the club. She was a beautiful, statuesque woman of German and Jamaican descent. Her caramel-colored skin was flawless, and her eyes were hazel. Clients would jokingly warn others that she had the ability to hypnotize you. Her body was the desire of all the male patrons and the envy of many women. And although David is now very generous with her, he was initially a tough nut to crack.

"Here you go – your favorite, Mr. Fontaine" the waitress said. David's favorite drink, a Bullet in the Head, contained vodka, rum, tequila and gin. There were many people would be astonished by David's drinking, because he was such a fitness fanatic. But despite his staunch bravado, he was not one to face his demons sober. And David had plenty of them to face.

"Well, it's about damn time!" David said.

"Sorry but the…" she began to explain, but he interrupted her quickly.

"Sorry, sorry…that's all I've been hearing all day" he said mockingly. "I'm so sick of apologies – just do it right the first time! Is that too much to ask for?!" he said, raising his voice. Disturbed by the shouting, the other patrons looked his way, but they quickly turned away when David notices them. Again, David's reputation preceded him everywhere. His tone and agitation caught Diamond's attention as well. "Hey, sweetie, listen… I have some things to take care of in the back… but I'll be back soon," she said, walking away swiftly. She knew that it would be best to leave him alone, let him have a few drinks; hopefully he would calm down. David just sat there, watching her walk away.

After soaking in the shower for an extended period, Lisa dried off, put on a nightgown and lay in the bed. While lying there, she began to pray to God. "Please Lord, help me with this situation, my marriage, – please help me God. Please help David. You know his heart, you know deep down inside he's a good man. You know he's been through so much. Please give me back the man I married, please… please…" She began to weep. Feeling emotionally and physically drained, she fell into a deep slumber.

At the Palace, the music was extremely loud, all the club lights were flashing, and the tables were adorned with glassed drinks and seductively glad woman. Superficial expressions of pleasure were written on the sea of faces. The multitude of hands reached within their pockets to pay for the services rendered. David had just finished his fourth Bullet in the Head, when Diamond tentatively approached him. "Hey, baby, you feeling better?" she asked seductively. "Look, don't ask me any questions, just sit right here and do what I pay you to do" he said with a slight slur. It was obvious that the Bullets in the Heads had taken their toll on him.

David grabbed Diamond by the arm and pulled her onto his lap. But Diamond flinched, because his grip was pretty tight. "Ok baby… I am… but baby… please, my arm… you're hurting me" she said pleadingly.

"Damn, woman, you're whining already! Shut up and just do what you're told! Can I find a woman that just does what the hell she's told!" he said, shouting. His shouting quickly got the attention of one of the bouncers. But Diamond signaled the bouncer to stay away. "Okay, sweetie, listen… you know I got you, and I'll do whatever you want. But you know management is watching, so we have to play the game, right?" she pleaded flirtatiously.

David, not one to submit to intimidation or authority, ignored her pleas. "Look, I don't care who the hell is watching, I drop a lot of money in this damn place. So I expect to get what I want. Do you understand that?!" he said threateningly. When David reached to touch Diamond's breast, she reluctantly backed away. "Sweetie… please… management is around," she said pleadingly. But David continued to ignore her pleas and reached to touch her again. This time, however, the bouncer walked over to intervene. "Excuse me, Sir, but you know the rules – keep your hands by your side, and please don't touch the dancers," the bouncer requested politely. But David, due to his staunch arrogance and his alcohol consumption, ignored this request. As he reached to touch Diamond again, the bouncer grabbed his hand and stopped him.

"Get your hands off me! Do you know who I am!?" David said condescendingly.

"Yes, I do, and personally I don't care who you are; so like I said, keep your hands off the dancer!" the bouncer said, raising his voice. By this time, the verbal altercation had drawn several bouncers to the scene, and the manager was summoned as well.

"Excuse me, but what seems to be the problem here, guys?" the manager asked, not knowing as he spoke, that it was David Fontaine, he was addressing.

"Hey, boss, it's Mr. Fontaine – he's just getting a bit out of hand, that's all. But it's nothing we can't handle," one bouncer responded. They'd all had problems with David in the past, and they were all itching to get their hands on him.

"Mr. Fontaine?!" the manager asked, reluctantly.

"Yes, it's me! Now tell your goons to back off" David said angrily.

"Ah... let's just calm down, Mr. Fontaine...and what seems to be thc problem?" the manager asked.

"Well, sir, Mr. Fontaine here ah..." a bouncer said, before abruptly being interrupted by David. "The problem is that you need to educate your toy cops as to who I am, that's the problem! I will shut this damn place down, do you hear me! Shut it down!" David continued to shout.

"Mr. Fontaine... please... calm down, sir!" the manager pleaded. The manager told one of the bouncers to call David a cab, which infuriated David even more. "I don't need a damn cab! I have a car!" David exclaimed.

"Sir, you have been drinking a bit, so we just want to make sure you get home safely," the manager said with concern.

Suddenly, David calmed down, and as he stood there, he circled the club with his head and looked at the sea of faces witnessing the scene. He placed his hand over his face, in an effort to cover up his embarrassment. "I'm sorry... I'm... really sorry..." he said in a whisper, shaking his head from side to side. He turned towards Diamond and took a step towards her, but the bouncers immediately positioned themselves between them. David clenched his fist and assumed a bellicose posture. But, he quickly shook it off and begins to walk towards the exit. The manager, still concerned for one of his best clients, offered the cab again, but David refused.

Lisa; awakened from her sleep and noticed that David was not in the bed. She quickly looked at the clock and saw that it was past midnight. She got out of the bed and walked around the house calling for him, but there was no response. Concerned, she grabbed her cell phone and called him. As David walked drunkenly towards his car, his cell phone rang. And as he struggled to get it out his pocket, it stopped ringing. His voicemail took the call.

He managed to open his car door and slumped onto the driver's seat. He pushed the voicemail and speaker button on his cell phone and laid his head on the steering wheel. "David… it's me" the soft voice said. When he heard her voice, his face began to gleam and he stared at the phone, hoping to see her beautiful face talking to him. "Lisa… my baby" he whispered. Lisa continues. "I'm just wondering how you're doing… please call me and just let me know you are fine… okay? Okay… please call me… I… love you." Lisa's message ended there.

Lisa, still fatigued and emotionally drained, lay back in the bed and began to pray again. "Please Lord…

just let him be okay… please… keep him safe… and… bring him home." As she continued to talk to God, her petite and exhausted body fell fast asleep again. A woman of strong faith, she had always tried to leave things in God's hands.

Meanwhile, his skills impaired by the alcohol, David slowly drove down Pierce Street. He had avoided driving for many years on this street. On it, an edifice had profound significance to him. As he continued driving with a sense of trepidation, it suddenly appeared before him: the Jerusalem House of God Church, the church that David and his mother attended when he was a child.

His mother, a devout Christian, would take David to church, despite his father's opposition – his father, a very successful lawyer as well, was also an alcoholic, and was also prone to violence and abuse when under the influence. Still, despite the dysfunction, nothing unraveled their lives more than when David's mother was diagnosed with terminal cancer. After she passed away, David's father sunk deep into a pit of depression, and his alcohol abuse worsened. Consequently, David was left harboring a lot of anger and bitterness not only towards his father, but towards God as well.

David pulled into the parking lot of the church and parked his car right in front of the entrance. As he stared at the entrance, he began to reminisce about the times when he and his mother would walk through those doors. He could see her standing there, adjusting his attire, and reiterating the proper conduct for the house of the Lord. David smiled reluctantly at the thought. Then suddenly, consumed with emotions, he began to cry as he looked to the heavens. "Why?... she was so young… why did you take her from me?!... WHY?!" he yelled, raging at the heavens. Losing his mother to cancer and his father to alcohol caused a profound fear of abandonment in him.

And although his father is alive, they have been estranged for many years now.

Suddenly, David noticed a figure approaching the door of the church from within. He quickly wiped his tears and attempts to focus his eyes. When he finally managed to focus, he recognized Pastor Flecha. Pastor Flecha had been the spiritual leader and Pastor of the church since David was a child. The Pastor recognized David's vehicle because he had seen David in it before, although it had been awhile since he has.

"David...! David!" the Pastor shouted hoarsely. He was in his eighties, and his health had been failing. But David looked at the Pastor briefly, backed his car out and sped off. David knew what the Pastor was going to talk to him about and he wanted no part of it. It was not the first time David had parked outside the Church. Reestablishing his relationship with God and going back to church was not something David wanted anything to do with at this time.

He was still angry with God for the loss of his mother – and anger is something David relishes holding on to.

David pulled his car into the driveway of his home. He got out his car and, still impaired by the drinking, stumbled a bit on his way to the door. As a struggle ensued between David and the lock on the door, Lisa was awakened by the noise. The window in their bedroom faced the driveway, so she peeked out to ensure that it was David. When she saw his car, she released a sigh of relief, knowing that he was fine. She was fully aware of David's pattern of drinking alcohol when he became angry or stressed. Knowing that he was out driving under those conditions gravely concerned her.

Lisa heard that David was still struggling with the door and that concerned her as well. Earlier, that had been an issue that sparked his anger. Therefore, she decided it was best to go down and open the door for him.

But when she began to walk towards the bedroom door, the struggle stopped, and David was successful in opening the door. However, the slamming of it quickly followed that. "Damn door!" David shouted. Lisa struggled with the decision: should she go downstairs and meet him, or should she wait until he came up? She decided to wait for him upstairs, hoping that by the time he came up, he might have calmed down a bit.

David went to the kitchen, opened the refrigerator, and pulled out a carton of orange juice. Not bothering to get a glass, he drank out the carton. When he was done, he put the juice back and began to walk towards the stairs.

When Lisa heard him coming up the stairs, she decided to hop back into bed. She felt it would be best to allow David to think she was asleep, in the hopes that he would go to sleep as well. He was always better to talk to when he was well rested, and especially when he wasn't drunk.

David, opened the door of their bedroom while Lisa lay in the bed, motionless. Drunk and tired, he slumped on the bed beside her. It was not long before she began to feel David's hands caressing her body. "Hey… baby… Hey… wake up" he said with a slur. Lisa, knowing that David was trying to initiate some intimacy, ignored his plea. This was a common practice for him when he drank, but it was one Lisa did not approve of. She did not like to make love to her husband when he was drunk. "Lisa! Hey, wake up!" he said, raising his tone. Lisa decided to respond verbally, at least, so she turned her body around to face him.

"Hey… baby, please… just go to sleep, it's late – we can do this some other time…ok?" she said reluctantly. David did not like to be rejected.

"Some other time?! I want you now, Lisa, not some other time!" he said angrily. As he spoke, Lisa suddenly smelled an aroma that she recognized from the past, an aroma that had ignited some serious altercations between them before. It was the distinguishing aroma of Diamond; it was the dancer's perfume. And if there was anything that could quickly eradicate Lisa's patience and passive demeanor, it was that. It quickly infuriated Lisa.

"I know I do not smell this again, David!" she said threateningly.

"What are you taking about, woman?" he said defensively.

"This perfume on your clothing! Were you with that damn woman again David?! Tell me, were you?!" she asked angrily.

"Look… just make love to me…I don't want to talk about that right now" he said pleadingly.

"I'm not touching you! You think I want to make love to you… while I smell another woman's scent on your body! You must be crazy, David!" she said, angry and disgusted.

Lisa quickly got out of the bed and began to walk out the room. Suddenly, she felt David snatch her by her hair. "Get the hell over here! You're my wife and you will do what I tell you!" he said angrily.

"David…please let me go…please you're hurting me!" she pleaded loudly.

"Shut up! Just shut up!" he said. He began to rip away at Lisa's clothing as she continued to scream and plead for help. "David! Please, no, DAVID… DON'T DO THIS… NO!" Lisa screamed. David went into an explosive rage and began to hit Lisa repeatedly. "DAVID, NO!" Lisa continuously pleaded for him to stop, but to no avail. David was determined to have, what he felt was rightfully his, even if he had to take it.

Javier thought he was dreaming when he heard the sound of someone banging on his door. When the banging continued, however, he quickly realized that he was not. Looking at his clock, he noticed that it was 3:00am. Of Javier, a person of medium height who was somewhat thin and had "average" looks, one thing could be said for certain: he epitomized the meaning of a true friend. He was compassionate and selfless, so when someone needed a shoulder to lean on, he was often their first choice. In addition to being Lisa's best friend, they were co-workers as well.

The loud banging at his door continued. "Wait up; I'll be right there!" Javier shouted. "Who could this be at this time?" he asked himself.

"Javier, please open the door – Javier, please!" the voice shouted in desperation. Javier immediately recognized the voice: it was Lisa. He opened the door. "Oh, God, Lisa, not again!" he said in disbelief.

Without hesitation, Lisa ran into his arms and said, "I'm sorry, but I don't know who else to turn to." She began to sob and shake uncontrollably.

Her face was covered with bruises and her left eye was beginning to shut completely due to the swelling. Her once-beautiful lips were now distorted by blood running down the side of her mouth. "I need to take you to a hospital," Javier pleaded desperately. "Just give me a few minutes to get dressed," he added nervously. As Javier quickly turned towards his room, Lisa responded sharply, "NO! I mean, please… I don't need to go to the hospital; I'll be fine," she said almost apologetically.

"But, Lisa, he might have broken something!" he says, troubled. "Have you taken a good look at your face? Huh? Have you?"

He rushed to the bathroom and returned with a mirror. This was not the first time that Javier had seen this violence, and the beatings were getting more severe;

he was getting tired of it. "I don't think you have: just look at your face, Lisa, look!" he said sharply. When he raised the mirror in front of her face so that she could see, she gasped when she saw her reflection. She slowly raised her hand to her face and lightly brushed her wounds, as if making an effort to erase them. The beatings she had sustained from her husband in the past had never left such marks. As she continued to stare, her chestnut eyes, even though one was almost completely shut, could not stop the river of tears that began to flow. Lisa wiped her tears swiftly. "I'm so sorry, Javier; I had better go. I've inconvenienced you enough and on top of that, I've made you angry; I'm so sorry," she said.

"Look, I'm not angry. I, well...I guess I'm a little angry. It's just that I'm tired of seeing you go through this; you deserve better!" he said, raising his tone of voice. She approached him and hugged him tightly. "I don't know what I would do without you," she said with a slight chuckle. Obviously sensing Javier's anger, she tried to lighten the mood.

"You had better hope you never have to find out," he countered, with a slight chuckle of his own. Although Javier understood the severity of this issue, he reciprocated with humor. "Listen, why don't you crash here tonight; my floor is really comfortable."

"You would make me sleep on the floor, won't you?" Lisa giggled.

"Now, that's the way I like to see you: smiling and laughing," Javier said. "But, seriously, I would have peace of mind if you stayed here tonight," he said pleadingly.

"I guess you're right, Javi; anyway, your home is always so peaceful, in contrast to mine, which is full of so much torment and chaos," she said sadly.

"Well... I guess there are advantages to living alone," Javier answered uncertainly. He lifted his hand and gently placed it on Lisa's chin, turning her face from side to side. "You had better put something on that before you go to bed," he said with concern.

"Yeah, I guess I'd better; I can't go to work trying to look cute with a face like this, huh?" she responded sarcastically. Javier just looked at her and smiled halfheartedly. "You…ah, mind if I take a shower?" Lisa asked.

"Of course not; you know, mi casa es su casa," he said with a smile.

"Gracias," she retorted.

"I have a pair of pajamas you can use. Uh...why don't you go ahead, take a shower, and I'll get some ice and things for your face," he said as he went to retrieve the night clothes.

Lisa knew her way around Javier's apartment because this was not the first time she had used it as a "safe haven." She knew exactly where to get the towels and other necessities. As she entered the bathroom, she turned and called out to Javier. "Javi?" she called. "Javi" was an affectionate nickname she used for him. "Can you please get me those pajamas you mentioned?"

"Absolutely!" he replied. Javier proceeded to his bedroom and rushed back with the pajamas in his hand. "Here you go," he said as he handed them to her.

"Thanks! Oh! These are cute!" she teased.

"Hey! Watch it! I'm telling my mother that you laughed at the 'jammies' she brought me," he joked.

Lisa entered the bathroom, closed the door behind her, and began to take her shower. Javier went to the kitchen to gather some ice to place them on a face towel. He knew that Lisa loved to drink hot cocoa, so he prepared some for her. Only minutes had gone by when he turned around to see Lisa standing there. Though her hair was wet and her face was completely bruised, her beauty still could not be masked. Javier grabbed the cup of hot cocoa and the face towel.

"Follow me," he insisted softly. Lisa followed as he led her to his bedroom. He told her to please get into the bed and to sit up; she complied. "Here, drink this," he said as he handed her the cup. "Cocoa! Oh, thank you, Javier," she said with a smile. As she sipped the cocoa, Javier gently placed the face towel against her bruises, one by one. She flinched. "Oooh, I'm sorry sweetie," he apologized, not ever wanting to hurt her.

"That's okay," Lisa said. "I'm just a little sore."

"I'll try to be gentler," he said.

She placed the cup down on the night table beside the bed. Javier noticed her eyelids beginning to flicker open and closed; she was fatigued. "Are you going to be all right?" he asked.

"Yes… thanks so much, Javier," she said.

"You're welcome," he replied. Javier moved from the side of the bed and tucked Lisa in. He covered her body from neck to toe, leaned down, and kissed her on the forehead. "Good night, Lisa," he said tenderly. "Good night, Javi," she replied.

Javier turned and walked toward the door. As he reached to turn the light off, Lisa called out to him: "Javi."

"Yes, sweetie?" he said.

"Don't you want to know why, this time?" she asked him.

"No, baby; there's no reason for it." Javier flipped the switch, turning the lights off, and closed the door.

The next morning, as the sun began to peek through the window, the alarm clock awakened Javier. He reached over, tapped the snooze button on the alarm clock that he placed next to the couch, and began to stretch. As he sat upright and looked into the mirror facing the wall in front of him, he noticed that the door to his room was open wide.

"Lisa?" he called as he stood up. "Oh, Lisa," he repeated in a sing-song fashion. However, there was no response, and the small apartment did not allow much room for a sudden disappearance. Lisa was obviously gone. Lisa and Javier worked together, and Lisa was not due to arrive at work until 9:00 a.m.; it was only 6:00 am. Considering her past patterns, Javier suspected that Lisa had gone home, and that made him very upset. When Javier arrived to work, he quickly searched the offices for Lisa; it was obvious by his behavior that he was not in a good mood.

"Joyce, where's Lisa?" Javier asked abruptly.

"Well, good morning to you, too, Javier," Joyce replied sarcastically.

"Listen, I don't have time for games… I mean, hey, I'm sorry, Joyce – I just needed to talk to her," he said remorsefully. "That's okay. Well, I haven't seen her; I don't think she's come in yet," Joyce answered.

"Really? Are you sure? But, she's never late," he said with genuine concern.

"Well, maybe she's sick or something. Hey, everyone has a bad day every now and then, right?" she said.

"Yeah, everyone has a bad day... but not like this," he said in a low whisper.

"What'd you say?" Joyce asked.

"Nothing; just thinking out loud," he replied. "Listen, I am sorry for reacting the way I did earlier," he said. "By the way, where's Mr. Castro?" he added. "Maybe he knows where Lisa is."

"That's okay. Like I said, everyone has bad days," Joyce alleged. "However, if I see her, I will let her know that you are looking for her. And Mr. Castro, well, he's not in today, so when the cat's away, the mice will play," she said humorously. Joyce was clearly trying to lighten up the mood a bit.

"Thanks," he said in frustration. As he started to walk away, Joyce called to him in a whisper.

"Javier, Javier," she called quietly.

"Yes," he responded.

"Listen, I know this is none of my business, but do you and Lisa have something going on?" she asked, with an air of anticipation.

"WHAT!" he said, obviously offended by the question. "Why is it that a man and a woman can't have a great relationship without people thinking they're sleeping with each other – damn!" he said sharply. "And yes, you're right; it's none of your business," he said.

"Hey, easy now; I'm your friend, remember? In fact, I'm friends with both of you. I've just never seen you act like this. Is everything okay?" she asked, with sincere concern.

"Yes, Joyce; everything is fine. And, again, I'm sorry; it's just not been a very good day," he said unenthusiastically.

"No need to apologize, Javier. I'm equally concerned for her," she said softly.

"Really?" he asked. "Do you know what's going on?" Joyce's concern implied that she might be aware of the abuse Lisa had been facing. If so, then maybe she could help him convince Lisa to seek some help before this situation escalated, if it had not already done so. Joyce did not respond to Javier's question, and the look on her face gave the impression that she regretted making that statement. "Joyce, if you know something, tell me, please," Javier pleaded.

"Not here: these walls have ears. Come with me," Joyce said, as she grabbed Javier by his arm and pulled him away. She took Javier to an empty office, away from all possible eavesdropping. Once they entered the room,

Javier immediately shut the door behind them. He grabbed Joyce by the arms and asked her frantically, "Tell me, Joyce, what do you know? Is Lisa all right?"

"Hey, let me go! You're hurting me! Joyce said sharply. "Must you men put your hands on us all the damn time?! She told me that you were different; what's your problem, Javier?"

"I'm so sorry, Joyce; really, I'm so sorry. But I'm so worried for her right now. God, I hope she's alright," he said, beginning to weep. "You know, don't you? You know about the beatings, don't you?" he asked.

"Yes, yes I do, and I also know that you've always been there for her, because she told me so," she said. Javier continued to sob uncontrollably. Seeing this, Joyce reached out and embraced him tightly, trying to comfort him. "I hope she's okay; I don't know what I'd do if anything happened to her" he said as he tried to wipe away his tears. "It's not like her to just get up and leave like she did this morning without letting me know and on top of that, she hasn't even showed up to work," he said.

"Wait, she was at your house this morning? I don't understand. What was she doing there?" Joyce asked. Javier broke away from Joyce's embrace and walked toward the window in the office. "Javier, talk to me. What was she doing in your house this morning?" she asked again.

"He hit her again, and this time it was worse then ever. I tried to convince her to go to the hospital, but she wouldn't listen… just like always," Javier said desperately. Joyce tried to comfort Javier as he reflected on Lisa's condition when she arrived at his home.

Meanwhile, at the LIONS DEN Gymnasium, the sweat dripped profusely down David's face. His physique was imposing, standing over 6'3" and weighing a muscular 250 pounds. Despite his workout, his hair remained in place, his eyes intent and piercing. His facial features were chiseled and reminiscent of a perfectly carved statue. These physical characteristics were very appealing to Lisa. Despite his youth at only 33 years old, he was already a highly respected lawyer and a senior partner in a very successful law firm. He and Lisa had been married for over 4 years, and although it began like a fairy tale for Lisa, it had turned out to be a nightmare. Despite past evidence of his abusive tendencies, many turned a blind eye to it, due in part to his "prestigious" status and his success. After finishing his last set, it dawned on him as to where Lisa might have gone this morning and where she might be at that moment. He reached into his gym bag and pulled out his cell phone. He stepped outside to find a secluded area, so that no one would hear his conversation, and dialed Lisa's number.

At the Lincoln Memorial Hospital, Lisa was waiting for the results of her X-rays when she heard her cell phone ring. She looked at her caller ID and noticed that it was David calling; she decided to ignore his call. David reached her answering machine.

"Hi, you've reached Lisa. Please leave your name and number and I will get back to you. Thank you and have a blessed day!"

David left a message. "Hi, baby. Listen: I'm sorry about this morning. I'm worried about you... please call me," he said. He hung up the phone and headed back to go inside the gym. In addition, although the message he left her gave an impression of remorse and concern, he was more upset then anything. He contemplated calling her job, but considering what had happened, he did not want to stir up any suspicion or alarm if she was not there.

As he was opening the door to the gym, a man inadvertently bumped into him on the way out. "Hey, idiot! Do you mind?" David angrily said to the man.

"Hey, relax; sorry, I didn't mean to bump into you," the man responded.

"Well, just be more careful next time – damn," David said.

"Okay, man, I don't want any problems," the man responded. It was obvious that the man did not want to squabble with David, so he just walked away. David, on the other hand, was looking for someone or something to vent his frustration on.

David entered the men's bathroom and locked the door behind him. He reached into his gym bag and pulled out a small kit. When he opened the kit, it revealed several syringes, loaded with steroids. Always looking for a way to excel and set himself apart from his contemporaries, his excessive use of the steroids had become an addiction. He took one of the syringes and injected it into the side of his buttock. Given his innate controlling and aggressive attributes, the side effect of the steroids exacerbated things even more.

Back at Lisa's job, Javier's emotions were more subdued. He was still visibly upset and concerned about Lisa, and his concentration suffered. Despite the fact that Javier could not call Lisa on her cell, his concerns were compelling him to ignore that. Lisa and Javier had been friends for a very long time, since long before she had even met David. Yet though Lisa attempted to maintain her relationships with both Javier and David, it was to no avail. David's controlling and jealous nature would not allow Lisa to have any male friends. Initially, Javier made a honest attempt to befriend David, but consequently he stopped trying.

Joyce could sense the anger and concern in Javier's voice, so she decided to approach him in an effort to comfort him. Suddenly, Javier turned around and said desperately, "You know what? I don't care. I'm calling her right now!" But just as he reached inside his pocket to get his cell phone, it started to ring. He saw that the caller ID showed that it originated from Lincoln Memorial Hospital. "Joyce… Joyce! It's Lincoln Memorial! Oh, God! I hope it's not about Lisa!" he exclaimed. Reluctant to pick it up for fear he would get some tragic news; he paused and looked at Joyce. "Pick it up, Javier, pick it up!" she said urgently. However, he would not. "Give me that!' she said. "Hello, hello!" she yelled frantically.

The person replied, "Hello, who's this? Joyce? Is this you?" the female voice said.

"Yes, it is – is this you, Lisa?!" Joyce responded with joyful relief.

"Yes, girl, it's me," Lisa said sadly.

"It's Lisa?" Javier asked loudly and exhaling in relief. It was wiser for Lisa to use a public phone when calling Javier, because of her husband's disapproval of him. As he began to reach for the phone, Joyce immediately gestured him to wait. "Girl, what's up? What is going on? We're worried sick about you!" Joyce said excitedly.

"Calm down, girl; please why you're always shouting? I've had enough drama for the day," Lisa said. "I'm fine, just a little… hey, where's Javier, and why did you pick up his phone?" Lisa said curiously.

"Girl, he's right here, but I don't know if you should talk to him, because he's really upset!" Joyce said.

"I bet he is. Please put him on," Lisa said quietly.

Torn between his relief that they had finally heard from Lisa and the fact that he was still upset, Javier reached for the phone. "Hello" Javier said, trying to stay calm. "Hi Javi– before you start to say anything, please let me explain, okay?" Lisa asked contritely.

"Go ahead," he said.

"Well, I couldn't sleep because my emotions were riding high, plus I thought I should take your advice and go to the hospital, and..."

Before Lisa could finish, Javier interrupted her. "But Lisa, you should've awakened me or...." Lisa quickly interrupted as well. "Javi, you said you would let me explain, so please, please, I don't need you to be angry with me also," she said, beginning to sob.

"Please don't cry, Lisa; I'm sorry... but, please understand, I was so worried, and all these crazy thoughts were going through my mind," he told her.

Joyce broke in: "Is she alright?" Javier quickly nodded and signaled that she was ok. Continuing with the conversation, he said "Listen, what's most important right now is that you're fine, and I'm so relieved to hear from you, Lisa. I love you, Lisa," he said with conviction. Javier and Lisa had exchanged those words rather platonically in the past, but Javier had never said it with the profound intent that he just did. You see, unknown to Lisa, Javier was in love with her. However, he always knew that he was never "her type," so in his mind, he accepted the reality that they could only have a friendly relationship. Nonetheless, his heart was not in the same accord with his mind.

"I love you, too, Javi, and I'm sorry I worried you. Here I was, trying to take care of business without imposing on you again, and I just made it worse. Maybe David's right," she said sadly.

"WHAT!" Javier responded with astonishment. He immediately looked at Joyce, who was gesturing to him to calm down; he complied. "Lisa, what are you saying, 'David is right' – about what?" he asked calmly. Joyce realized that they could use some privacy, so she excused her self. Before leaving, she told Javi to tell Lisa that she would talk to her later. Javier complied, but quickly returned to his conversation with Lisa. He was very curious to know what Lisa meant by her statement about David. "So tell me, Lisa, what you meant by 'maybe David is right,?" he asked again.

"About everything... you know, he said that I'm immature and that I'm always doing things that piss him off, so maybe it's true. I mean…look what I've done to you," she said with disillusionment.

"Listen, you're not immature. If anybody's immature, and obviously has other problems as well, it is David, and there's no excuse for what he does, none, so I don't want to hear you talk that way, Lisa. I won't have it!" he said firmly. Feeling himself getting upset, but understanding how fragile Lisa was at the moment, he took a deep breath and toned it down. "But listen, sweetie: what's most important right now is your health and your physical condition. So what did the doctors say?" Javier asked. The fact that Lisa continued to go back with David after going through several similar episodes was really upsetting to Javier. However, his love and concern for her superseded everything else at this moment.

"Well, I'm still waiting for the results of the X-rays, but they don't think it's that bad." Lisa responded. In actuality, the doctors suspected that her cheekbone could very well be broken, but she did not want to alarm or anger any Javier more than he was already.

Suddenly a voice caught Lisa's attention. "Excuse me? Excuse me? Mrs. Fontaine?" a nurse asked.

"Yes ma'am, that's me," Lisa replied.

"Mrs. Fontaine, the doctor is ready to see you to go over the results of your X-ray. Please come this way," the nurse said.

"Javi, I have to go; the doctor is ready to see me now. But listen, I promise to call you later, okay?" she said, trying to calm him.

"Okay, sweetie; do you want me to come there?" he asked. "No, Javi… really; I'm fine and I promise that I will call you soon," she said.

"Okay, please don't forget, because I won't be at peace until I hear from you," he pleaded.

"I won't forget, baby; promise, kisses, bye," she said.

"Back to you, baby, bye," he said.

The X-ray revealed what the doctors had suspected: Lisa's left cheekbone was broken. She had a loose chip on the corner near her eye socket. Although it was currently stationary, it was susceptible to movement, so she would eventually require surgery to have the chip removed. The doctor told her that she had come very close to having severe or even permanent damage to her eye. The doctor, who was very familiar with these sorts of cases, strongly recommended that she press charges. Yet although this had been recommended in the past, she always had refused to do so. Concerned about some other possible internal injuries, the doctor recommended some additional blood work and tests, which she submitted to. They released her and told her that they would call her when the results of the tests were in.

After a long day at the hospital, Lisa was extremely fatigued and in need of much rest. In addition, although she preferred not to go home, she felt compelled to do so.

David's impatience and anger was growing stronger, since plenty of time had gone by and he had not yet heard from his wife. Realizing the severity of his actions, he took a deep breath and called her again. The phone rang once. Lisa looked at the phone's caller ID and saw that it was David. Despite her reluctance, she picked it up. "Yes, David!" she said angrily.

"Oh God, I'm so glad you picked up, baby; I've been so worried about…"

Lisa quickly cut in. "Don't baby me! Do you know what you've done to me? This time you've gone too damn far!" she sobbed. "But, you know what? This will be the last time you put your hands on me, so help me GOD!. I'm done, finished with you and this marriage… it's been a living hell!" she yelled.

"Baby, you don't mean that! Listen… I will get help… I promise," he pleaded.

"No, that's what you always say, and you never follow through, David; no, enough!" she finally said, defiantly. "I'm just going to swing by the house and pick up some things and we can sort everything else out later. Expect to get some papers real soon! Goodbye!" Lisa hung up.

David looked at his phone with utter disbelief. Lisa had never responded to him in this manner. He was used to her succumbing to his manipulation and distorted authority. David looked at his phone and mumbled, "We'll see."

It was the end of the normal business day, and right when Javier was about to get into his car, his cell phone rang; it was Lisa. "Hey, Javi, how are you?" "I'm so glad you called!" he answered her, joyfully.

"I'm done, Javi; I'm done with David and this marriage," she said, with regret in her voice. "I tried to make it work, you know. I was raised to believe that you only do this once, and so… I tried… but I'm scared, Javi, I'm really scared this time!" she said.

"Sweetie, I know you did, I know… but you're doing the right thing; you'll see," Javier said in an encouraging tone.

"I know, and I should've listened to you a long time ago. I'm sorry," she said apologetically.

"It's okay and there's no need to apologize. It had to be your decision and nobody else's," he said.

"Well, listen, I need a huge favor, Javi, but I promise not to impose on you for too long," Lisa began.

"Yes beautiful, and I want you to know that you're never imposing on me, but hey, you know that already," he said, trying to hide his elation. Javier's joy obviously came from the fact that he was ecstatic that Lisa had decided to leave David. "So tell me, I'm at your service!" he said.

"Well… I was wondering if it would be ok for me to crash at your place… until I can find an apartment, of course… and I promise not…"

Before Lisa could finish her sentence, Javier responded. "Yes, of course you can. When do you want to move in?"

"Well, today…is that too soon?" she asked reluctantly.

"Of course not, baby!" he replied.

"Okay, great, but one more thing," she said.

"Name it," he replied.

"Well, I'm going to go to the house to pick up some things, but I want to take as much as I can so that I won't have to go back there any time soon. But I don't have much space in my car, so I was wondering if you could meet me there so I could load some things in your car as well?" she asked.

"Are you on your way now?" he asked, and she told him she was. "Okay, great! Well, I'll just need to stop and get some gas and buy some things from the grocery store, because I don't have much at the house. I should be there within an hour or so; is that ok?" he asked.

"Oh sure; that's perfect, because that will give me some time to put some things aside before you get there!" she said excitedly.

"Great, baby, I'll see you there!" he said.

"Okay Javi… uh… Javi?" she asked.

"Yes baby?" he replied. "I really appreciate this, sweetie; you're a God-send, and I love you so much!" she said.

"You're welcome, Lisa, and I… love you, too," he said quietly. Javier knew that the love that Lisa felt for him was not the same as what he felt for her. However, just to have her near him and away from the abuse at the hands of her husband was enough for him – for right now.

David was furious, and his possessive and controlling nature did not tend to accept defeat easily. After Lisa hung up on him, he decided to go to a bar to have some drinks. However, instead of lessening, his anger grew stronger after every drink. In addition, there were all these reprehensible thoughts rushing through his mind.

"Mr. Fontaine?" the bartender called. David was deep in thought and did not even hear him. "Mr. Fontaine?" the bartender called again.

"What!" David finally responded loudly.

"Sorry, sir, but can I get you anything else at this moment?" the bartender asked.

"No, and just leave me the hell alone!" David shouted.

"Okay, sir, no problem, sorry," the bartender replied. "In fact, just give me the… well… the hell with the bill. This should cover it; I'm out of here!" David said angrily. He placed a one-hundred dollar bill on the bar and started to walk out. Noticing that he was staggering a bit, the bartender became concerned about his driving in that condition. On the other hand, he was familiar with David's temper, so it was with reluctance that he asked: "Sir… can I call you a cab?" David, insulted by the insinuation, quickly turned around and walked toward the bartender. The bartender backed away as David got closer. "Do I look like I need a damn cab? Huh?" he said loudly and angrily.

"Well…I just was trying to…" the bartender started to reply, but David cut him off.

"What're you trying to do?" David yelled. "Why don't you try minding your own damn business?!" he added, in an intimidating tone. The silence in the bar became deafening as the patrons in the bar looked on mutely. David's imposing size and reputation were not to be taken lightly. Finally, to everyone's relief, David walked out. By the time he got to his car, the thought of Lisa leaving him – and, more importantly to him, the thought of the humiliation he would suffer – increased his anger to the boiling point. Furthermore, he was determined not to allow it to happen. He suddenly remembered that Lisa said that she was going to go to the house to pick up her belongings. Hurriedly he started the car and sped off to meet her there.

Meanwhile, while Javier was checking out at the grocery store, he decided to call Lisa to let her know that he was on his way. Lisa answered the phone. "Hola, Javi; are you on your way?" she asked.

"Wow, you sound chipper! I even get some Spanish! I haven't heard you speak it in awhile; I thought you had forgotten it," he joked.

"Ha, ha; somebody's got jokes," she replied with a chuckle. "You just need to hurry up so that you can help me load all this stuff."

"I know, baby. I'm on my way. I will be there very soon," he replied. "Okay. Well, let me go so that I can continue stacking this stuff, and then we can load up and get out of here." Suddenly, she became quiet. Javier noticed the change. "Are you okay, sweetie?" he asked with concern.

"Yes, baby. In fact, I haven't felt this good in a very long time. I was just wondering why it took me so long to make this decision," she replied.

"Yes, I know, but what's most important is that you finally did," he said.

"You're right. Okay, well, I will see you soon, baby; drive carefully," Lisa said.

"Okay, I will!" he replied. Once they hung up, Lisa's phone rang again. When she looked at the caller ID, she saw that it was from Lincoln Memorial Hospital, but in an effort to hurry, she ignored the call.

Despite his condition and his reckless driving, David arrived quickly at the house. He immediately saw Lisa's car parked in the driveway. To obstruct her ability to drive off, he parked his car directly behind her. He climbed out of his car and slammed the door behind him. Hearing the car door slam, Lisa smiled, assuming that it was Javier. But the sudden jiggling of keys and the unsuccessful attempts to open the door implied otherwise. It quickly dawned on her that it could not be Javier. She quickly peeked outside the window and saw

David's car in the driveway. David began to bang on the door, shouting, "Lisa, open the damn door!" Lisa immediately began to shiver in fear and quickly reached for her phone. Knowing that Javier was on his way, she hit the speed dial and called him.

Javier answered the phone. "Okay baby, I know I'm running…" Javier started to say, but was immediately interrupted by Lisa. "Javi! Oh, God, Javi! Don't come here! David is here, and…" she attempted to say quietly. But before she could finish, David knocked the door open and began to shout for Lisa. With Javier still on the phone, Lisa began to scream and run upstairs. "Lisa, baby, are you alright? What's going on? Please answer me," Javier pleaded.

"Javier, it's David. He's here and he's real upset, and, I think he's drunk, so don't come here. I don't want you involved in this!" she pleaded.

"What, are you crazy?! I'm not going to leave you there alone with him, especially after what he did to you! No, Lisa, I'm almost there!" he shouted.

"But Javi, I…" Lisa started to say, but before she knew it, David appeared before her. "Who are you talking to? Tell me, you slut! Who is it?" David said angrily.

"Give me that damn phone!" he said. David snatched the phone away from Lisa and began to shout into the phone.

"Who is this? Talk to me, you punk!" he said. However, there was no response. Javier had hung up. As David threw the phone against the wall, he grabbed Lisa by the arm and slung her against the wall, too. "Is that the kind of man you like, a coward that won't face me, huh, tell me, is that what you like?!" he asked her repeatedly.

"Stop, David, please; let me go, you're hurting me," she pleaded and sobbed. As Lisa tried to stand, he threw her back down to the ground, wrapping his hands around her neck. He began to choke her. "No one will have you, Lisa, you hear me, no one!" he said in an evil tone as he continued to choke her.

As Lisa desperately tried to free herself, she could feel her life slipping away, since her tiny body was no match for his strength. Suddenly, the sound of someone's voice resounded loudly throughout the house. "Let her go!" it said. Startled, David released his stranglehold on Lisa and turned around. He was surprised to see who it was.

"You! What the hell are you doing here?" David said. Although Lisa was almost incoherent due to the loss of oxygen, she was able to recognize who it was and quickly shouted, "JAVI!"

"Yes, sweetie; are you alright?" Javier asked desperately. David looked at Lisa and said, "You must be kidding! Are you cheating on me with this? Why you lil…"

David lunged at Javier and a fight ensued. Javier, though small in stature, relied on his speed and agility to maneuver his way around David. "Lisa, go! Run out of the house now!" Javier shouted. Lisa tried to get up, but still feeling weak, and reluctant to leave Javier, she froze.

Suddenly, David grabbed Javier and wrestled him to the ground, pinning him down in the same manner that he had Lisa. He wrapped his hands around Javier's neck and began to choke him. "Do you think you're man enough to take her from me, huh, do you?" David asked angrily. "She's going to watch you die, you little piece of…" "Let him go, you animal; let him go!" Lisa shouted. Lisa was able to retrieve a large pan from the kitchen and she struck David with it with all of her strength.

The blow forced David to release Javier; unfortunately, it only stunned him. Although he never lost consciousness, it infuriated him even more. "You are both going to die for this, both of you!" he screamed angrily. He ran down the steps toward the kitchen. It was obvious that the blow to the head and his drunken state impaired him only somewhat. At that moment, Javier managed to get up, grabbed Lisa by the arm and started to lead her down the stairs. When they got to the bottom of the stairs, they faced David, coming at them with a knife in his hand. As he charged at them, Javier and Lisa ran and managed to get through the front door and to the outside.

"Where are these damn cops? I called them before I got here!" Javier said desperately. Fortunately, David, still weakened, stumbled to the ground. Just as he tried to get up, the police arrived, sirens blowing and lights flashing. Lisa and Javier quickly began to run toward the patrol car as they pleaded for help. "Please help us, please! My husband has a knife!" Lisa cried. "Okay Miss, you're fine now; we're here," the officer shouted to her.

But just as the police officer turned his attention from Lisa, he noticed that David was still coming toward them with the knife still in his hand. "Sir, stop right there and put the knife down!" he commanded David.

Nevertheless, David kept coming, shouting obscenities at Lisa. By this time, several patrol cars had arrived at the scene, and the officers were prepared for anything, weapons drawn and at the ready. David stopped, but he never dropped the knife. "Sir, it's all right; we don't want this situation to escalate, so please, put down the knife so that we can talk," the officer said in a softer tone.

"Do you know who I am, huh? I'm David Fontaine!" David shouted at the officer. "And nobody does this to me and gets away with it; they have to pay!" David started to walk toward Lisa and Javier while they stood behind the patrol car.

"Sir… Mr. Fontaine! Don't come any closer or you will force us to shoot you!" the officer said with reluctance.

"Lisa, come to me right now! You're my wife… come here!" David shouts. Lisa looked at Javier as if she were looking for advice from her dear friend. But surprisingly, Javier stared at her silently. He knew that this had to be Lisa's decision.

David started to run toward them. The noise from the police officer's weapons rang like a fourth of July celebration for about two minutes before David fell to the ground. When the gunfire ceased, there was a deafening silence for a brief moment, but soon afterward, you could hear the wallowing screams and sobbing of a woman.

It was Lisa. "NOOOOOOOOOOO, NOOOOOOOOO, OH GOD!" she screamed. Despite everything, seeing her husband riddled by a barrage of bullets was too much for Lisa to bear. Obviously in shock, she collapsed in Javier's arms. "LISA, LISA!" Javier shouted. "Please! Somebody help her!" he shouted. They rushed Lisa to the closest hospital: Lincoln Memorial.

Despite the drama that he had just experienced, as well as his close brush with death, Javier was there as always, vigilant by Lisa's side. The doctors and hospital staff tried to encourage him to leave, but he refused. The doctor administered a battery of tests, and at the outset, everything looked fine, but they were still waiting for some other results. They gave Lisa a sedative to calm her down, so she slept for a short time. But eventually she was showing signs of awakening, and Javier noticed. "Baby, sweetie… it's me, Javi; are you ok?" he asked softly. "Javi... Javi... please tell me I had a bad dream, tell me it isn't true," she said in a whisper. "Is he dead, Javi? Did they kill him?" she asked desperately.

"Yes, baby, yes... I believe he is," he answered reluctantly.

Despite Javier's feelings for Lisa, he understood: she loved this man. Moreover, it was going to be very difficult for her to live with what she had seen. Javier, still concerned for her welfare, pressed the call button for the nurse. "Yes?" the voice said.

"She's awake...can you please come check on her?" he asked pleadingly.

"Yes, sir, I'll be right there," the nurse replied.

The nurse arrived with the doctor and they checked her vital signs; all looked well. "Mrs. Fontaine, all looks..." but before he could finish, Lisa interrupted. "Please, doctor, please... call me Lisa," she said – the invoking of her husband's last name was too painful at this time.

"Ah… yes, ma'am, sorry. Well, everything looks very good; in fact, everything appears great!" the doctor said. "Your blood and urine tests came back normal, and most importantly, the sonogram revealed that the baby is fine as well!" he said enthusiastically.

Lisa and Javier looked at the doctor in astonishment.

"Baby?…you're pregnant?" Javier asked with disbelief." Lisa spoke at the same time: "There must be a mistake, doctor; I'm not pregnant, I… mean, I didn't know," she said, obviously in shock. She quickly turned back to face the person that she always sought solace from – Javier. However, this time, he was equally shocked and at a loss for words.

"Well… ma'am, in fact, the records showed that you were here earlier today and that somebody was supposed to have called you, and..." Before the doctor could finish his sentence, Lisa began to shake. She screamed uncontrollably "NOOOOOOO!"

Javier tried to comfort her, but he could only stand by while the doctor and nurses tried to calm her down. They were obviously concerned that another emotional trauma might cause harm to her and her baby. Not wanting to take any chances, the doctor gave her a sedative. Under normal circumstances, the news of the baby would have brought joy and happiness to her ears. But the immediate thought of having a child by the man that she had been leaving, and who was now deceased, was just too much for Lisa. Nevertheless, like so many times before, there was no doubt as to who would be there for her – and, now, for her baby. As Javier stood before Lisa, he gently brushed her hair back into place with his hands and kissed her on the forehead. As he stared at her beautiful face, he pulled a chair close to her bed and sat down beside her. He grasped her left hand gently, then leaned close to her ear and whispered, "I'm here, sweetie, so don't you worry, I... will be here for you, and your baby... always. I love you."

A nurse arrived to talk to Lisa, but Javier, standing by her side, met her. "Oh... is she asleep?" she asked Javier.

"Yes.... yes, it's been a very difficult night for her," Javier responded.

"Yes, I heard...it's all over the news!" she exclaimed. "Is it true?!" she asked shockingly. "What is?" Javier replied somberly. "That he tried to kill you guys?" she said. "Yes...yes, it's true." Javier replied. "Well, I don't know how she's going to react to the news" she said with uncertainty.

"What news?" Javier asked.

"The news about her husband," she said.

"Oh…she already knows. I told her earlier that he died," he said sadly.

"Died? You mean... you didn't hear?" she asked, astonished.

"Hear what?!' Javier asked impatiently.

"He's alive! Her husband is alive!" she said in disbelief.

"But it can't be…I saw him get shot…several times!" he said, raising his voice.

"Hey! I can't believe it myself! I mean, he was practically dead when he arrived here! But… hey… I guess it wasn't his time," she said reluctantly.

As the nurse began to walk out of the room, Javier looked up to the heavens and then looked at the sedated Lisa in utter disbelief.

The End!

To be continued……

Quality of Your Love

As defined by Webster's, Quality can refer to the characteristics or essence of achievement or excellence, or it can mean excellence itself. We see it written on the labels of almost every garment we use, the food we consume, the cars we drive, and the homes we live in. It amazes me that more often than not, we spend more time looking for and buying a "quality" product than we do in finding "quality" love. I used to question and debate to no end when someone would tell me that they loved me, but their actions, in my mind, showed me otherwise. However, I now realize that they truly believed they did and that debating them was a lost cause. So now what I evaluate and question is the "quality" of the love. I understand that there are times, due to circumstances, when we can only afford to have used items; items that might have dents, scratches, tears, and/or discolorations. However, can we afford to do that with love – and if we

can, should we? As human beings, we are flawed. Consequently, our hearts and minds may have some of the characteristics of "used" items. And the love we give and allow ourselves to receive may be flawed as well. However, it does not have to be and it was not meant to be that way. We have the ability to improve our education, skills, and jobs in an effort to position ourselves to have better-quality items, and quality of life. We spend countless hours, and not to mention huge amounts of money, in training to do so, don't we? Moreover, we can do the same with our minds and hearts. It does require God's help and a spiritual "rebirth," if you will, but it can happen. So no, we do not have to settle for a "used" love – one filled with inadequacies, deception, and ongoing disappointments. The love we give and receive should be of the very best quality: a love filled with honesty, loyalty, and

commitment. A love that upholds the standards set before us by our creator over our own. You see, any consumable or non-consumable item that is manufactured is INSPECTED and APPROVED before it is sold. Any "reputable" company wants to sell and/or provide the best-quality service/or product. If they do not they will eventually fail, and go out of business. So... I ask you. Is the love you are giving and/or receiving failing you? Are you going "out of business?" If so, maybe it is time that you give it a thorough inspection. And since we are flawed and fallible creatures, I would strongly recommend that you ensure God approves it!

Forgiveness

In Ephesians 4:32 (NASB) God says: *Be kind to one another, tender-hearted, FORGIVING each other, just as God in Christ also has forgiven you.* Yet oftentimes, forgiveness can perpetuate the condoning of certain behaviors. That is not its purpose. Some people use forgiveness as a "green light," so to speak, for premeditated nefarious behavior. If the individual is not liberated from the behavior, you must evaluate how it is affecting your life, especially in terms of your spirituality. In Matthews 5:29 (NASB) God says: *If your right eye makes you stumble, tear it out and throw it from you; for it is better for you to lose one of the parts of your body, than for your whole body to be thrown into hell.* Consequently, everyone you allow into your life becomes part of your body. Thus, we must evaluate our relationships with those we have allowed in our lives. And

sometimes we must "cast aside" those we have forgiven and still love.

Domestic Violence

It is estimated that every year in the United States, approximately 3 million women are assaulted by their partners. One in four women in the U.S. will be assaulted by their partners over their lifetimes.[I] In 2001, according to the United States Census Bureau, there were 691,710 non-fatal domestic violence acts committed and 1,247 fatal incidents of domestic violence. In homes where domestic violence occurs, children in the home are at a 300% greater risk of being abused.[I] According to Southern Connecticut State University: "In 95% of family violence cases, the victims are women who are beaten by male partners. In 1% of the cases the reverse is true. There are an estimated 28 million battered women in the U.S., more than half of all married women in the country. In the U.S., one woman is beaten by her husband or partner every 9 seconds. Battering is the

single major cause of injury to women between the ages of 15 and 44 in the U.S., causing more injuries than car accidents, muggings, and rapes combined. 70% of the assault victims seen in the emergency room of Boston City Hospital are women who have been attacked in their own homes. 3 out of 5 women in the U.S. will be battered in their lifetime." Domestic Violence Facts

Women are just as likely as men to engage in partner aggression.

Source: United States Census Bureau

For additional information, please contact the National Domestic Violence Hotline at 1-800-799-7233.

www.ingramcontent.com/pod-product-compliance
Ingram Content Group UK Ltd.
Pitfield, Milton Keynes, MK11 3LW, UK
UKHW020135250726
13967UKWH00002B/662